WHAT'S ALL THE BUZZ ABOUT?

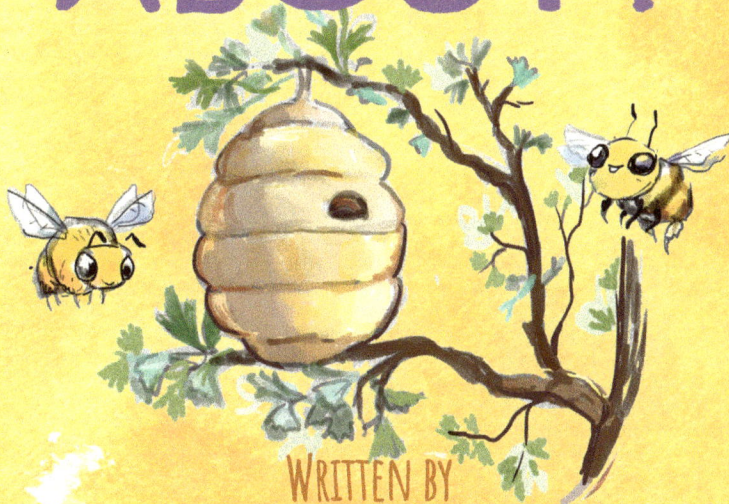

Written by
Marta L. Cramer

Illustrated by
Marta Maszkiewicz

Halo
PUBLISHING
INTERNATIONAL

Halo
PUBLISHING
INTERNATIONAL

Halo Publishing International
7550 WIH-10 #800, PMB 2069,
San Antonio, TX 78229

First Edition, September 2024
ISBN: 978-1-63765-640-2
Library of Congress Control Number: 2024914223

Halo Publishing International is a self-publishing company that publishes adult fiction and non-fiction, children's literature, self-help, spiritual, and faith-based books. Do you have a book idea you would like us to consider publishing? Please visit www.halopublishing.com for more information.

Inspired by their farmers' market and honeybees.
www.ktfmproducts.com

KTFMproducts.com
Branchport, NY
(315)694-2934
Mail & Marta
3554 Darby's Corners Road
Branchport, NY 14418

To my husband, who has been the most avid supporter of my desire to write a book, especially about the importance of bees and our beloved market.

4

Hi! I'm Harriet the Honeybee! Welcome to Keuka Trail Farm Market.

Did you know that honeybees like me are very important for children, adults, flowers, and animals?

Yes! We are important to you!

There are so many interesting facts about honeybees that I bet you did not know. For example, we are flying insects that collect nectar and pollen; we can fly between fifteen and twenty miles per hour. That's fast!

The honeybee is also the only insect that produces food for humans, which is honey.

Have you ever tried honey? It's my favorite food!

2 ATENNA

4 WINGS

Thorax

Abdomen

EYE

Head

Feeler

6 LEGS

8

This is Theodore. He is a male bee, which is also called a drone.

One interesting fact about drones is that they don't have a stinger; only female bees have stingers. Except for that, all the other parts of male and female honeybees are the same. We have a head, a thorax, and an abdomen. We also have three pairs of legs, a pair of antennae, and two pairs of wings.

Did you know that the honeybee also has an exoskeleton? This means that, just like you, we have a layer of protection for our organs, similar to your rib cage.

Are you afraid of bees? Have you ever been stung?

Don't worry! We are generally nice to people, but if you get too close, we may need to protect our home. That's why, when you see people near us, they may be wearing suits.

When there are a lot of bees in one area, it is called an apiary. This is where some of us are raised. Sometimes, to calm us down, they use a smoker.

Nectar is the sugar produced by plants. Honeybees use this nectar to make honey. One worker bee can produce one-twelfth of a teaspoon of honey in her lifetime. This means it takes twelve honeybees to make one teaspoon of honey. All worker bees are female.

Pollen helps us become strong and stay healthy, so we can have more honeybees. When we collect the pollen, it helps the plant to produce fruit or vegetables, so people have something to eat. This is called pollination.

Can you see the pollen that is collected by honeybees?

Honeycombs are very important to bees. The honeycomb is a place where the bees can store the pollen, as well as the honey that is made.

How many sides does each opening in a honeycomb have? Did you say six? Correct! That's also the shape of a hexagon.

Wax is made from the honeycomb.

There are four stages in the life cycle of a honeybee. They are the egg, the larva, the pupa, and the honeybee.

The honeycomb is also used as a "Nursery" for honeybees. Specific nurse bees work during the larva stage. They feed it to help it grow. They also make sure the hive stays clean.

Can you imagine not being able to eat your favorite fruit for breakfast?

If we didn't have bees, many fruits and vegetables would not grow. Honeybees pollinate 80 percent of all flowering plants.

It's up to us to make sure honeybees stay around for a long time.

Ways to Protect Honey Bees

❀ Grow flowers and plants that honey bees like.

❀ Don't use chemicals that can hurt honey bees. Be careful what you use to get rid of weeds and unwanted bugs. Pesticides hurt the honey bee. Instead, find other ways to get rid of pests.

❀ Remember, honey bees won't sting you unless they feel threatened. So, next time you look at a flower or a plant, see if you can find a honey bee. Don't interrupt her; just watch her. Please do not hurt her.

Glossary

Abdomen of a Honeybee—Contains vital organs, including, stomach, and stinger.

Apiary—Large enclosure for colonies of bees in bee hives.

Colony—Where honeybees live together.

Drone—Male bee.

Exoskeleton—Hard, outer covering that protects the honeybee's internal organs.

Honeycomb—Where honeybees store pollen, honey, and honeybee eggs; its openings, or cells, are six-sided.

Nectar—Sugary fluid inside flowers.

Pesticides—Substances that are used to control pests.

Pollen—Fine powder substance, mostly yellow, from a flower.

Pollination—Method by which honeybees help flowers, fruits, and vegetables grow. Collection and transfer of nectar and pollen from plant to plant.

Thorax—Midsection of honeybee; segment between head and abdomen.

Wax—Used by honeybees to construct their home, where young bees are raised and honey is stored.

www.ingramcontent.com/pod-product-compliance
Lightning Source LLC
Chambersburg PA
CBHW060800150426

42813CB00058B/2774